Butler, Gwendoline.

Death lives next door.

10/92

$16.95

DATE			

003520 054939